Common Core Lessons & Activities: Inventors and Inventions

By Carole Marsh
Published by Gallopade International, Inc.

Printed in the U.S.A. (Peachtree City, Georgia)

TABLE OF CONTENTS

G: Includes Graphic Organizer
GO: Graphic Organizer is also available 8½" x 11" online download at www.gallopade.com/client/go
(numbers above correspond to the graphic organizer numbers online)

Who Is an Inventor?

Read the text and answer the questions.

An inventor is a person who makes something that did not exist before. Inventors also like to improve existing ideas or inventions. Although an invention is often the result of a single inventor's work, it also can be the result of a team of people. Inventors are usually curious. They like to know how things work. Inventors must be creative. They tend to look for new ways to solve today's problems. Inventors are often persistent. This means they try again, even after they fail. It might take years to perfect an invention so inventors also have to be hardworking.

The thing that the inventor makes is called an invention. Inventions are often created to solve a problem. For example, someone invented a candle because it was dark and he or she needed to see. Inventors also might make an invention because they wish to do something more efficiently or quickly. The automobile allows people to travel from one location to another more quickly and without the struggle of walking or riding a horse.

Inventors change the way we work, travel, and communicate. For example Orville and Wilbur Wright forever changed history by inventing the first manned aircraft to actually fly! Alexander Graham Bell's telephone allowed people to communicate over long distances, and Tim Berners-Lee developed the Internet we use today, allowing people to access information and entertainment with a simple click.

1. A. Define inventor as it is used in the text.
   B. List at least three characteristics of an inventor.
   C. For each characteristic, explain why it is important to the invention process.

2. Match the following questions to whether they are best answered by paragraph 1, 2, or 3 of the text.
   A. ______How do inventors affect our lives?
   B. ______What are the common characteristics of an inventor?
   C. ______Why do inventors invent?

3. List three inventions not mentioned in the text. Give examples of how each invention affects your daily life.

PROBLEM-SOLUTION-RESULTS

Why Invent?

Read the text and follow the instructions.

Inventions usually solve a problem or allow people to do something more quickly or efficiently. Some inventions improve upon a previous invention. For example, ancient peoples used an invention called a "sundial" to measure time. However, sundials were usually large, heavy, and not practical for carrying from place to place. Sundials did not work properly in cloudy weather!

Instructions: Complete the graphic organizer by identifying the problem each invention solved and any further improvements that have been made to the invention.

Problem

Spears

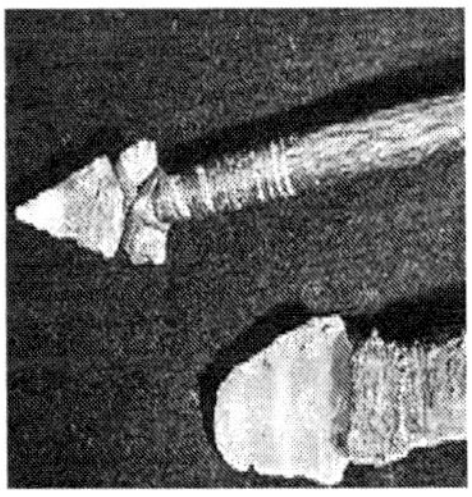

Improvements

Problem

Sundial

Improvements

Problem

Quill and Ink

Improvements

Agricultural Inventions

Read the text and answer the questions

Before 1794, slaves on cotton plantations painstakingly picked cotton and removed the seeds by hand. In 1793, Eli Whitney observed this difficult process on Georgia plantations. He thought there must be a better way to remove the cotton seeds.

In 1793, Eli Whitney invented the cotton gin. The cotton gin is a machine that separates seed and unwanted materials from cotton after it has been picked. The cotton gin was automatic, meaning it required little human work to operate. With Whitney's cotton gin, a plantation could remove seeds from 55 pounds of cotton per day—a great improvement!

Whitney thought he could sell his cotton gin to plantation owners, so he patented his invention in 1794. A patent is a legal document that protects an invention or idea from being stolen or copied. But, plantation owners and other businessmen copied Whitney's invention without permission, and Whitney sold very few of his patent cotton gins.

Copies of the cotton gin became immensely popular on Southern plantations because they increased cotton production. As a result, cotton plantations became more successful and needed more and more slaves to pick the cotton. From 1790 to 1808, Southerners imported approximately 80,000 Africans. Because the cotton gin greatly increased slavery in the South, the cotton gin is considered one of the many causes of the American Civil War.

1. What agricultural problem did the cotton gin solve?
2. A. Define patent as it is used in the text.
   B. Why is it important to patent an invention?
3. Explain how the cotton gin affected each thing listed below:
   A. Southern plantation owners
   B. Number of slaves in the South
   C. Eli Whitney
   D. The production of cotton
4. Why is the cotton gin considered one of the causes of the Civil War? Cite evidence from the text to support your answer.

Before 1834, farmers cut and gathered grains by hand. Cutting grains by hand was a slow and difficult process. Farmers could only plant as much grain as they could later cut and gather. In the early 1800s, many inventors attempted to create a mechanical reaper that was automatic, requiring little human effort.

Cyrus McCormick's father designed a mechanical reaper, but it never worked correctly. After his father's death, Cyrus McCormick, and his slave Jo, improved his father's design. They built a reaper that was pulled by a mule and automatically cut and gathered the grains. McCormick first showed his working mechanical reaper in 1831.

Working independently, a man named Obed Hussey designed and patented a similar mechanical reaper in 1833. McCormick did not patent his invention until around 1834.

With his new patent, McCormick started the McCormick Harvesting Machine Company. McCormick cleverly advertised his mechanical reaper and showed farmers how to use his invention. Because McCormick was a smart entrepreneur, his mechanical reaper became an international sensation, unlike Obed Hussey's reaper, which went out of business. McCormick was later elected to the French Academy of Sciences "as having done more for agriculture than any other living man."

5. How did the mechanical reaper improve agriculture?

6. A. Use the texts to define automatic.
   B. What is the benefit of inventing an automatic machine? Cite evidence from both texts to support your answer.

7. Use the text to compare and contrast Eli Whitney and Cyrus McCormick in terms of success and the impact of their inventions.

Eli Whitney **Cyrus McCormick**

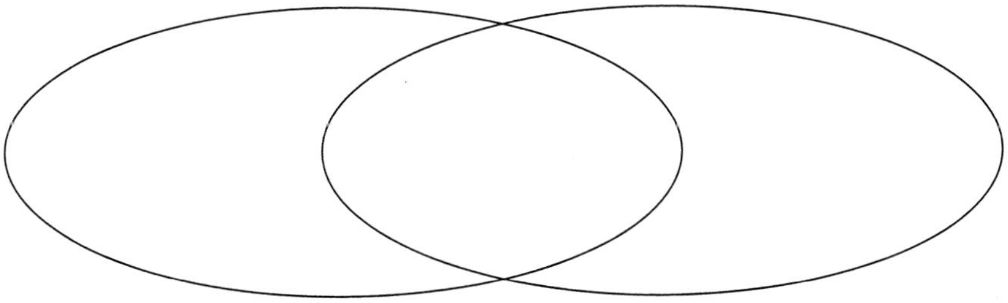

8. Why is Cyrus McCormick remembered as the inventor of the mechanical reaper and not Obed Hussey?

A Medical Breakthrough

Read the text and answer the questions.

In 1921, Franklin Delano Roosevelt contracted polio. Polio is a virus that causes the loss of control of body parts, or even death. Like many other people with polio, Roosevelt became paralyzed from the waist down. During his presidency, Franklin D. Roosevelt fought the disease and eventually died from polio in 1945.

In the 19th and 20th centuries, polio became an epidemic, affecting hundreds of thousands of people in Europe and America. In the early 20th century, polio was considered the most frightening and dangerous disease in America. By 1950, scientists around the world were looking for a solution to this terrifying disease.

In 1952, medical researcher Dr. Jonas Salk developed the polio vaccine. The polio vaccine did not cure the disease, but it protected people from ever getting the disease. Dr. Jonas Salk's polio vaccine was slowly given to more and more people around the United States each year as protection against the disease. As a result, the number of people affected by polio decreased each year.

Number of Polio Cases in the U.S. from 1950 to 2000

Yr	1950	1952	1954	1956	1958	1960	1970	1980	1990	2000
No	33,300	57,879	38,252	15,140	5,787	3,190	33	9	6	0

1. A. What problem did Dr. Salk's invention address?
   B. What solution did Dr. Salk's invention present?
2. Describe the effects of polio on President Roosevelt.
3. Which dictionary entry accurately defines epidemic as used in the text?
   A) an isolated occurrence of an infectious disease
   B) the widespread occurrence of an infectious disease
4. According to the data, when was the U.S. polio epidemic at its worst?
5. What caused the change in number of polio cases? Cite evidence from the text to support your answer.
6. Predict the number of polio cases in the year 2020. Explain.

By Boat, By Rail

Read the text and answer the questions.

In the late 1700s and early 1800s, the steamboat and steam locomotive greatly improved transportation in the United States.

American inventor John Fitch used a steam engine to power a boat. He patented the first steamboat in 1791. Fitch's steamboats carried passengers and cargo, but his boats were not successful because they were too slow.

Another inventor, Robert Fulton, soon built a steamboat that was faster and more efficient. In 1807, Fulton's steamboat, the *Clermont,* made history when it traveled from New York City to Albany in 32 hours at an average speed of 5 miles per hour. By 1814, Fulton was running his steamboat business on rivers and lakes near six large cities. Fulton's steamboats were not only used for transporting people, they transported livestock and crops from the Midwest to the East.

Steam engines were also used to power the first locomotives. When railroads became popular in 1828, short railways were built across the South. Steam-powered locomotives brought Southern cotton to the seaports for shipping to Europe. Railroads were built to link agriculture in the South and Midwest to factories in the North. Railroads encouraged people to travel and do business in different parts of the United States. In 1869, the Transcontinental Railroad was completed, allowing people and goods to travel across the United States with much greater ease.

1. What was the primary goal of early transportation inventions?
2. Describe the role of the steam engine in the development of the steamboat and the steam locomotive.
3. Explain how the steamboat and steam locomotive affected each of the following.
   A. movement of goods
   B. movement of people
   C. connection between regions of the U.S.
4. In what ways did the steamboat and steam locomotive compete with each other?

PRIMARY SOURCE ANALYSIS

First Flight

Read the texts and answer the questions.

After three years of experimenting with gliders, the Wright Brothers made history. On December, 17, 1903, at Kitty Hawk, North Carolina, Orville Wright flew the first flying machine powered by a lightweight gasoline engine. It rose to 10 feet and landed heavily after 12 seconds. The brothers made three flights that day. The longest lasted 59 seconds and covered 850 feet.

"My brother and I became seriously interested in the problem of human flight in 1899 ... We knew that men had agreed that human flight was impossible. To say something was impossible, people often said, "It can't be done; a man might as well try to fly." We were encouraged by the idea that different insects, fish, reptiles, birds and mammals were flying every day at pleasure. Therefore, we though it reasonable to suppose that man might also fly... We decided to write to the Smithsonian Institution and inquire for the best books relating to the subject.... We found that men of the very highest standing in the profession of science and invention had attempted to solve the problem of human flight... But one by one, they had been compelled to admit failure. In studying their failures we found many points of interest to us."

— notes written by Wilbur Wright (paraphrased)

1. What problem did Wilbur and Orville Wright attempt to solve?
2. Describe 5 steps of the process by which the Wright Brothers made the first successful flight.
3. A. How can studying another person's failures help an inventor?
   B. Why is it important to think differently from other people?
4. Identify at least three positive characteristics that made the Wright Brothers successful inventors. Cite evidence from the texts to support your answer.
5. Were Orville and Wilbur Wright afraid of failure? Cite at least three examples from the texts that support your response.

ORDERING EVENTS

Transportation & Progress

Read the text and answer the questions.

Transportation is essential to our everyday life. However, getting from place to place was not as easy in the past as it is today. Before machines, people relied on natural forms of transportation, including their own two feet. Other forms of natural transportation include riding on horseback or paddling a canoe.

The first improvements to transportation used simple mechanical devices. A bicycle, for example, still uses the natural power in a person's legs, but it is faster, and it requires less energy to travel the same distance as a person walking. Wagons and carriages pulled by horses allowed whole families to travel together without walking.

Technology continued to improve, and so did transportation. The steam engine was an invention that made travel by animal power unnecessary. If given fuel, the steam engine never tired, never got sick, and could work day and night. The steam engine was used in the first steamboats and locomotives.

Today, gasoline engines have replaced most steam engines. Gasoline engines require less fuel and allow people to travel at incredible speeds for greater lengths of time without stopping.

1. Use the text to number each of the following modes of transportation in the correct progression of invention:

   A. ____bicycle
   B. ____walking
   C. ____motorcycle

   A. _____propeller plane
   B. _____space-ship
   C. _____jet plane

   A. ____horseback
   B. ____automobile
   C. ____horse-drawn wagon

   A. _____steamboat
   B. _____canoe
   C. motorboat

2. List at least 3 ways engines are an improvement over natural power.

3. Write a journal entry describing what life would be like without engines for transportation. How would you get to school, to the store, or even to another state?

Electricity Was the Spark!

Read the text and answer the questions.

Benjamin Franklin was a famous scientist, inventor, and statesman in the late 18th and early 19th centuries. In Franklin's most famous experiment, he flew a kite in a storm with a metal key tied to the string near his hand. When lightning struck the kite, the electric current ran through the kite string to the metal key. Franklin concluded that electricity could be controlled and directed.

American scientist Thomas A. Edison invented over 1,000 inventions during his lifetime, but his most famous invention is the light bulb. Benjamin Franklin's discovery about how electricity moved gave Edison an idea. Using metal wires, Edison conducted electricity through a thin metal filament that became hot and glowed brightly—the first light bulb! By the time Edison died in 1931, entire cities were lit by electric bulbs!

Other scientists continued to study electricity using Franklin's ideas. English scientist Michael Faraday discovered that moving a magnet inside a wire coil could produce electricity. He went on to invent the first electric motor. Improved versions of Faraday's invention are used in millions of electric devices today! Over the years, many devices powered by electricity were invented—including air conditioners, refrigerators, electric stoves, computers, and many other useful devices.

1. Make inferences from the text to determine whether each statement is **true** or **false**. Rewrite each false statement to be true.
   A. _____Benjamin Franklin invented electricity.
   B. _____Inventors rarely build upon the work of other inventors.
   C. _____Discoveries about the natural world can lead to useful inventions.

2. What is the relationship between all three inventors?

3. Write a short narrative titled "When the power goes out" and describe the challenges you might face if the electricity suddenly turned off. Think about the inventions in your home and school that require electricity and identify alternative solutions if the power goes out.

Why Invent?

Read the quotations and answer the questions.

> Necessity is the mother of invention.
>
> –Plato, Greek philosopher

> I don't think necessity is the mother of invention. Invention, in my opinion, arises directly from idleness, possibly also from laziness—to save oneself trouble.
>
> –Agatha Christie, British novelist

1. A. Summarize the point of view of the first quotation.
   B. Summarize the point of view of the second quotation.
2. What is the relationship between the two quotations?
3. What is the difference between a "necessity" and "saving oneself trouble?"
4. Which quotation do you most agree with? Why?
5. In your opinion, why were each of the following items invented—because of a need, or because of laziness? Give reasons and evidence to support your opinion.
   A. fork B. television C. telephone D. reclining chair
6. As a class, discuss and debate your responses to the questions. Expand your answers to the questions based on the discussion.

Inventors & Their Inventions

Complete the graphic organizer by identifying each invention and how it changed the world.

Inventor	Invention
Alexander Graham Bell	
Willis Carrier	
Thomas Edison	
Henry Ford	
Robert Fulton	
Joseph Glidden	
Charles Goodyear	
Cyrus McCormick	
Samuel F. B. Morse	
Dr. Jonas Salk	
Eli Whitney	
Wilbur & Orville Wright	

How It Changed the World

CAUSE & EFFECT

Ford and the Assembly Line

Read the text and answer the questions.

Many people believe Henry Ford invented the automobile, but he did not. Henry Ford did, however, change how automobiles were made. Putting together a car was a difficult task. Ford wanted to make cars more quickly, so that they cost less and he could sell his cars at a cheaper price.

In 1913, Ford invented the moving assembly line. Using a process called "division of labor," Ford divided the process of putting together an automobile into 84 separate steps. Workers at Ford's factories laid the car parts in the order they would be needed. As the cars moved along the assembly line, each worker added one specific part. A worker could complete his single step quickly, without learning the entire process.

The moving assembly line and division of labor reduced the time it took to assemble a car from 12 hours to approximately 30 minutes. The assembly line also allowed Ford to produce Ford Model T's more quickly and cheaply. Today, many products are produced using division of labor and the assembly line.

1. A. What did Ford invent?
   B. Why did he invent it?
   C. Describe the purpose of "division of labor."

2. Use the text to complete the graphic organizer.

Effects of Ford's Assembly Line

3. Analyze the quotation and explain the message or moral.

Ford quotation	Message or moral
"The man who thinks he can and the man who thinks he can't are both right."	

Inventions in the West

Read the texts and complete the graphic organizer.

In the early 1800s, a gun could only fire one bullet at a time. In 1836, Samuel Colt invented the "Colt Revolver." Colt's gun could hold six bullets at once. Thus, a person could shoot six times before needing to load the gun with more bullets. Colt Revolvers were used by the U.S. Army to help win the Mexican-American War because the Colt Revolver was fast, reliable, and accurate.

Colt's revolvers had several negative effects on Native Americans. U.S. pioneers and settlers used the Colt Revolver to hunt wild animals for food and to defend themselves from Native American attacks. In the 1870s, the U.S. military used the Colt revolvers to defeat many Native Americans in the Indian Wars.

In the late 19th Century, many American settlers moved west to the "open range." Settlers became farmers and ranchers with herds of cattle and pigs. Settlers quickly realized they needed fences to protect their land. Wooden fences were too expensive, and stone fences were impossible because there were not many large rocks on the flat, western lands.

Joseph Glidden invented barbed wire in 1874 and forever changed the West. The thin wire with sharp barbs was affordable and could easily divide large areas of land. Settlers used the barbed wire to divide the open range into sections of property. As a result, the West's open range was no longer "open." Native Americans who once hunted on the open range lost their land.

1. Write an appropriate title for each text to express the main idea.
2. Complete the table by identifying the problem, solution, and results presented in each text.

	Problem	**Solution**	**Results**
Text 1			
Text 2			

Inventor, Innovator, Entrepreneur

Complete parts A, B, and C.

*An **inventor** creates a new product or system.*
*An **innovator** improves upon an existing product or system.*
*An **entrepreneur** creates a business to sell a product or service.*

PART A: Individually or in small groups, select one of the products below. Use at least two online resources to answer the research questions below and at least three questions of your own.

Steam boat	***Coca-Cola***	***PC software***	***Telegraph***
1. John Fitch	*1. John Pemberton*	*1. Gary Kildall*	*1. Joseph Henry*
2. Robert Fulton	*2. Asa Candler*	*2. Bill Gates*	*2. Samuel Morse*

1. A. Describe the role of person #1 in the history of the product.
   B. Was he the inventor of the product, an innovator, or an entrepreneur?
2. A. Describe the role of person #2 in the history of the product.
   B. Was he the inventor of the product, an innovator, or an entrepreneur?

PART B: Organize the information into a visual or digital presentation. Summarize the life of each person as well as his role in developing the product. Include any historic photographs or illustrations related to the invention, inventor, innovator, or entrepreneur.

PART C: Give your presentation to the class. Be sure to use a formal tone and explain all photographs and illustrations. As each presentation is given, the class should complete the Venn diagram comparing and contrasting the characteristics of each person.

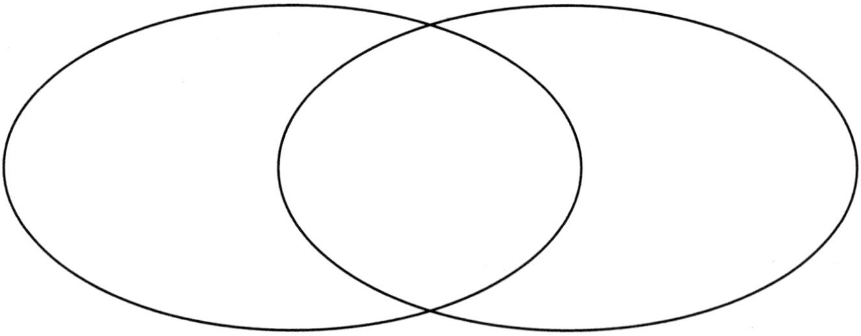

What Does It Take?

Use a dictionary or online resource to define each characteristic of an inventor, and explain why each characteristic is important to the process of inventing. Then answer the questions.

	Characteristic	Definition	How might it help an inventor?
A	creativity		
B	failure		
C	hard work		
D	persistence		
E	teamwork		

1. List at least 3 other characteristics an inventor might need. Explain.
2. Match each characteristic from the chart to the quotation that best describes it.
   _____ "Tis a lesson you should heed, try, try again. If at first you don't succeed, try, try again."
   _____ "To invent, you need a good imagination and a pile of junk."
   _____ "Two heads are better than one."
   _____ "Genius is one percent inspiration, and ninety-nine percent perspiration."
   _____ "Just because something doesn't do what you planned it to do, doesn't mean it's useless."

Communication Inventions

Read the text and answer the questions.

Language—We don't think about language as an invention, but it is. Long ago, people could not speak to each other. Over thousands of years, ancient people invented their own languages. Some civilizations, like the Ancient Egyptians, even invented symbols to write their languages on paper and stone. Written language allowed people to share ideas, knowledge, and instructions over long distances and to save information for future people.

Moveable Type Printing Press—Before the printing press, people wrote and copied historical, religious, and scientific information by hand. Johannes Gutenberg created a printing press that allowed a single book to be produced over and over very quickly. Gutenberg's printing press made many books available to many people who did not have them before.

Electric Telegraph—The electric telegraph sent messages over electric wires. By pressing a button, an operator could create patterns of dots and dashes. Samuel Morse created a code of dots and dashes for each letter of the alphabet. Morse Code allowed people to send written messages over long distances.

1. Why is language considered an invention?
2. How did Gutenberg's printing press improve written communication?
3. Identify the purpose of each invention in the text.
   ________________ To improve the spread of knowledge
   ________________ To communicate over long distances
   ________________ To provide a basic way for people to communicate
4. Complete the graphic organizer by identifying several communication inventions today that help us communicate.

PRIMARY SOURCE ANALYSIS

A Historic Experiment

The text is an excerpt from Alexander Graham Bell's journal.

Read the text and answer the questions.

Mr. Watson was stationed in one room with the receiving instrument. He pressed one ear closely against S and closed his other ear with his hand. The transmitting instrument was placed in another room and the doors of both rooms were closed.*

I then shouted into M the following sentence: "Mr. Watson—Come here—I want to see you." To my delight he came and declared that he had heard and understood what I said. I asked him to repeat the words. He answered "You said 'Mr. Watson—come here—I want to see you'." We then changed places and I listened at S while Mr. Watson read a few passages from a book into the mouth piece M. It was certainly the case that articulate sounds proceeded from S. The effect was loud but indistinct and muffled; If I had read beforehand the passage given by Mr. Watson, I should have recognized every word. As it was, I could not make out the sense—but an occasional word here and there was quite distinct. I made out "to" and "out" and "further" and finally the sentence "Mr. Bell do you understand what I say? Do—You—Un-der-stand—what—I—say" came clearly and intelligibly. No sound was audible when the armature S was removed.*

**M is a device for speaking into.*
**S is a device for listening.*

1. A. What event is described by the text?
   B. What is the historical purpose of recording this event?
   C. What is the scientific purpose of recording this event?

2. A. What is Alexander Bell's purpose for writing this journal entry?
   B. Describe the writing style Bell uses to narrate the event.
   C. List at least three elements of the text that help you "see" and "understand" the event.

3. According to the text, was the experiment successful? Cite evidence from the text to support your answer.

Radio & Television

Read the texts, analyze the photographs, and answer the questions.

Radio

AM and FM radio were invented by Edwin Armstrong in the early 1900s. Radio was "wireless" and quickly replaced wired telegraphs for carrying military information during World War I. Later, radio programs became a source of news and entertainment for families at home.

Television

Today, it is difficult to imagine life in America without the television. Philo Taylor Farnsworth invented the television in 1927. In 1947, very few U.S. families owned a television set. By the year 2000, approximately 98 percent of all American homes had at least one television. Television replaced radio as the main form of news and entertainment in the home.

Courtesy of the Library of Congress

1. A. What similarities do you notice between the two photographs?
   B. What differences do you notice between the two photographs?
2. What can you infer about the time period in each photograph? Cite evidence from the text to support your conclusions.
3. A. What advantage did the radio have that the telegraph did not?
   B. What advantage does television have that radio does not?
4. A. How have radios changed from the time in the photograph?
   B. How have televisions changed from the time in the photograph?
5. A. Besides radio and television, list at least 5 other sources of news and entertainment from the past or the present.
   B. Which source of entertainment or news do you prefer? Why?

Computers & the Internet

Follow the instructions for parts A and B.

PART A: Use what you know about computers to describe how a computer is useful for each of the categories.

Communication

Education

Entertainment

News

PART B: Read the quotations, complete the table by summarizing the main idea, and answer the questions.

Quotation	Main Idea
"A few generations ago, people didn't have a way to share information and express their opinions efficiently to a lot of people. But now, they do. Right now, with social networks and other tools on the Internet... people have a way to say what they're thinking and have their voice be heard."	
"Everyone is on the Internet but they're not talking with each other. There are groups upon groups out there but they don't talk to one another. So while the Internet brings everyone into a shared space, it does not necessarily bring them together."	

6. Do the quotations **support** or **contradict** each other? Support your response with evidence from the quotations.

7. A. In your opinion, is the Internet a useful tool for expressing your opinion? Why or why not? State your opinion and support it in a well-reasoned paragraph. Edit and proofread your work.
   B. As a class, discuss your responses.

Invent Something!

Follow the instructions in parts A, B, C, and D.

PART A: Most inventions try to solve a problem. Think of an everyday problem you might solve by inventing. Complete the graphic organizer.

Problem	Why is it a problem?	Who is it a problem for?

PART B: Think of an idea for an invention that will help to solve the problem. Use your imagination and be creative.

PART C: Describe your invention in the first box. In the second box, make a list of materials that you might need to make this invention. In the third box, draw what your invention might look like.

Describe It!	Build it!	Draw It!

PART D: Share your invention with your class. Explain what problem it solves, how it solves the problem, and who will benefit.

Inventing Process

Use a dictionary or other resources to complete the graphic organizer for each vocabulary word.

automatic	entrepreneur	inventor	problem-solving
design	experiment	mechanical	research
engine	invention	patent	testing

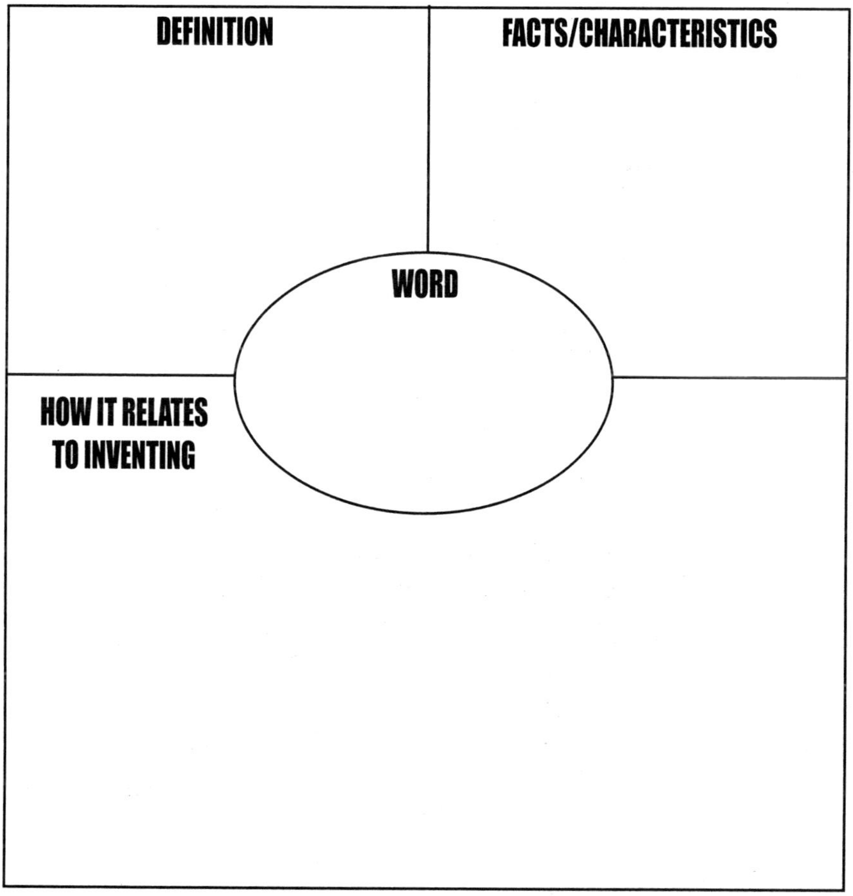

Correlations to Common Core State Standards

For your convenience, correlations are listed page-by-page, and for the entire book!

This book is correlated to the Common Core State Standards for English Language Arts grades 3-8, and to Common Core State Standards for Literacy in History, Science, & Technological Subjects grades 6-8.

Correlations are highlighted in gray.

PAGE #	READING *Includes:* RI: Reading Informational Text RH: Reading History/Social Studies	WRITING *Includes:* W: Writing WHST: Writing History/Social Studies, Science, & Technical Subjects	LANGUAGE *Includes:* L: Language LF: Language Foundational Skills	SPEAKING & LISTENING *Includes:* SL: Speaking & Listening
2	RI RH . 1 2 3 4 5 6 7 8 9 10	W WHST . 1 2 3 4 5 6 7 8 9 10	L LF . 1 2 3 4 5 6	SL . 1 2 3 4 5 6
3	RI RH . 1 2 3 4 5 6 7 8 9 10	W WHST . 1 2 3 4 5 6 7 8 9 10	L LF . 1 2 3 4 5 6	SL . 1 2 3 4 5 6
4-5	RI RH . 1 2 3 4 5 6 7 8 9 10	W WHST . 1 2 3 4 5 6 7 8 9 10	L LF . 1 2 3 4 5 6	SL . 1 2 3 4 5 6
6	RI RH . 1 2 3 4 5 6 7 8 9 10	W WHST . 1 2 3 4 5 6 7 8 9 10	L LF . 1 2 3 4 5 6	SL . 1 2 3 4 5 6
7	RI RH . 1 2 3 4 5 6 7 8 9 10	W WHST . 1 2 3 4 5 6 7 8 9 10	L LF . 1 2 3 4 5 6	SL . 1 2 3 4 5 6
8	RI RH . 1 2 3 4 5 6 7 8 9 10	W WHST . 1 2 3 4 5 6 7 8 9 10	L LF . 1 2 3 4 5 6	SL . 1 2 3 4 5 6
9	RI RH . 1 2 3 4 5 6 7 8 9 10	W WHST . 1 2 3 4 5 6 7 8 9 10	L LF . 1 2 3 4 5 6	SL . 1 2 3 4 5 6
10	RI RH . 1 2 3 4 5 6 7 8 9 10	W WHST . 1 2 3 4 5 6 7 8 9 10	L LF . 1 2 3 4 5 6	SL . 1 2 3 4 5 6
11	RI RH . 1 2 3 4 5 6 7 8 9 10	W WHST . 1 2 3 4 5 6 7 8 9 10	L LF . 1 2 3 4 5 6	SL . 1 2 3 4 5 6
12-13	RI RH . 1 2 3 4 5 6 7 8 9 10	W WHST . 1 2 3 4 5 6 7 8 9 10	L LF . 1 2 3 4 5 6	SL . 1 2 3 4 5 6
14	RI RH . 1 2 3 4 5 6 7 8 9 10	W WHST . 1 2 3 4 5 6 7 8 9 10	L LF . 1 2 3 4 5 6	SL . 1 2 3 4 5 6
15	RI RH . 1 2 3 4 5 6 7 8 9 10	W WHST . 1 2 3 4 5 6 7 8 9 10	L LF . 1 2 3 4 5 6	SL . 1 2 3 4 5 6
16	RI RH . 1 2 3 4 5 6 7 8 9 10	W WHST . 1 2 3 4 5 6 7 8 9 10	L LF . 1 2 3 4 5 6	SL . 1 2 3 4 5 6
17	RI RH . 1 2 3 4 5 6 7 8 9 10	W WHST . 1 2 3 4 5 6 7 8 9 10	L LF . 1 2 3 4 5 6	SL . 1 2 3 4 5 6
18	RI RH . 1 2 3 4 5 6 7 8 9 10	W WHST . 1 2 3 4 5 6 7 8 9 10	L LF . 1 2 3 4 5 6	SL . 1 2 3 4 5 6
19	RI RH . 1 2 3 4 5 6 7 8 9 10	W WHST . 1 2 3 4 5 6 7 8 9 10	L LF . 1 2 3 4 5 6	SL . 1 2 3 4 5 6
20	RI RH . 1 2 3 4 5 6 7 8 9 10	W WHST . 1 2 3 4 5 6 7 8 9 10	L LF . 1 2 3 4 5 6	SL . 1 2 3 4 5 6
21	RI RH . 1 2 3 4 5 6 7 8 9 10	W WHST . 1 2 3 4 5 6 7 8 9 10	L LF . 1 2 3 4 5 6	SL . 1 2 3 4 5 6
22	RI RH . 1 2 3 4 5 6 7 8 9 10	W WHST . 1 2 3 4 5 6 7 8 9 10	L LF . 1 2 3 4 5 6	SL . 1 2 3 4 5 6
23	RI RH . 1 2 3 4 5 6 7 8 9 10	W WHST . 1 2 3 4 5 6 7 8 9 10	L LF . 1 2 3 4 5 6	SL . 1 2 3 4 5 6
COMPLETE BOOK	RI RH . 1 2 3 4 5 6 7 8 9 10	W WHST . 1 2 3 4 5 6 7 8 9 10	L LF . 1 2 3 4 5 6	SL . 1 2 3 4 5 6

For the complete Common Core standard identifier, combine your grade + "." + letter code above + "." + number code above.

In addition to the correlations indicated here, the activities may be adapted or expanded to align to additional standards and to meet the diverse needs of your unique students!